Always Together at
Christmas

written by
Sara Sargent

illustrated by
Mark Chambers

Random House 🏠 New York

For my parents.
And ♥ to Jenna, my Swat superwomen, and Dan—who always believed.
—S.S.

For Jess: Thank you for all the support
and dog walks while I was doing this book.
—M.C.

The magic of Christmas is shared
from family to family,
from friend to friend.

Christmas will always mean love,

even if love feels
a little different this year.

Christmas is a time for family,

even if family gathers a little differently this year.

Christmas is something to believe in,

even if believing looks a little different this year.

Christmas is the season for giving,

even if giving happens in different ways this year.

Christmas is a light that won't be dimmed,
shining brightly,
illuminating the joy we share.

Cherish this Christmas.

Cherish the family and friends
who make it special.

Dream up new traditions,

and give thanks for each blessing.

Whether we fly, or drive, or walk, or call,

our cheer stretches across the miles.

No matter where we celebrate,

or how we celebrate,

we'll find a way to celebrate each other
on the most wonderful day of the year.

Because, no matter how far apart we are,

The Elves

Grammy 💜 Pop-Pop

Aunt P & Aunt J

Meow-y Christmas!

we're always together at Christmas.

Part of what makes each holiday season fun is creating new traditions. Whether your loved ones are all together or safely apart this year, try one of these ideas—or come up with your own!

 Send Christmas kits to family and friends, filled with DIY crafts and activities to do together over video.

 Deliver food baskets to your neighbors, especially elderly and at-risk people who can't leave their homes.

 Create a Christmas BINGO card and fill in squares with things like "bake cookies" and "watch a holiday movie."

 Rather than visit Santa at the mall, write him a letter or send him an email.

 Assemble a family advent calendar by putting Christmas wishes inside twenty-four little envelopes.

Throw your own Christmas concert at home and sing all your favorite Christmas songs.

 Make tree ornaments out of things like popsicle sticks, cotton balls, pom-poms, feathers, or pipe cleaners and send them to your loved ones.

 Host a virtual cookie decorating party, and swap recipes with friends or family members beforehand.